"Read it again, Grandad. Are you a sloth, Grandad? I love the pictures. They are funny. Is that a real monkey? Read it again, Grandad!"
Simon Howie, www.thescottishbutcher.com
(from Sophia, Jamie and Angus 4, 3 and 1.75)

"A wonderful book that is going to encourage children all over the world to love sloths and protect their rainforest home."
Dr Rebecca and Tamara, The Sloth Conservation Foundation, www.slothconservation.org

"As someone who loves all the same things as Simon – bagpipes, amber nectar and adventures around the world – I think you have created a sloth of impeccable character, inspirational determination and wonderfully Amazonian Scottish spirit. Simon is, of course, right. We must *always* seek to do what we love and be open to trying new things until we find our way in life."
Christian Grant, Education Support Edinburgh, www.ese.org.uk

"Who doesn't love the sound of bagpipes, or even the glories of the 'amber nectar', and where would this world be if it wasn't for the wonder of our natural world, adventure, music and harmony all sown together with a twinkle of fun! *Simon the Sloth* comes from an imagination that revels and abounds with such wonders and we would all be enlightened by reading and sharing Molly's enchanting story!"
Alasdair Hilleary, Loon Sporting Cartoons

"I thought it was really good and liked Simon playing his bagpipes in the rainforest best. I liked when he was in the rainforest and I liked every bit."
Leila and Romey Lyle, 7 and 4

"Molly has created a beautiful journey for Simon the Sloth to lead us on. A tale about why everyone should do what they love. It speaks to the childhood dreams in all of us. And of course we all need help from our own amber nectar from time to time."
Jonathan Agnew, Taybank Growers Cooperative, www.taybankgrowerscoop.com

Copyright © Molly Arbuthnott 2022
Illustrations Copyright © Maude Smith 2022

SIMON THE SLOTH

ISBN: 978-1-915439-41-3

Edit & layout Shaun Russell

Published by
Jelly Bean Books
Mackintosh House
136 Newport Road, Cardiff, CF24 1DJ
www.candyjarbooks.co.uk

Printed and bound in the UK by
Severn, Bristol Road, Gloucester, GL2 5EU

SIMON THE SLOTH

MOLLY ARBUTHNOTT

Dear Fergus
speed isn't everything!
Love,
Molly xxx

JELLY BEAN BOOKS 2022

Simon was a sloth but not an ordinary one. He played the bagpipes. He actually loved his pipes more than anything in the whole wide world!

The only trouble was that he could only play them slowly... so... so slowly! So slowly, indeed, that when he played them it sounded more like a cat yowling than an aspiring musician! He tried everything to speed up... He tried playing them swinging under his favourite palm tree.

He tried playing in the
Deep Atlantic Ocean...

He tried playing while sweating in the scorching heat of the Sahara Desert...

He tried playing surrounded by animals in the jungle…

He tried playing them while shivering at the top of Mount Everest...

He tried playing while eating a very hot spicy Indian curry in front of the Taj Mahal, but nothing seemed to work…

Poor old Simon! A big fat tear rolled down his furry face, followed by another and another.

After a further day of failed attempts, one of his sloth friends said,
"Here, have a sip of this. It will make you feel much better."
It was a funny looking orange liquid.
"What is it?" Simon asked.
"Amber nectar from your favourite palm tree," his friend replied.
Simon took one sip and WOW!

He was ZINGING! Zinging at one hundred and twenty miles an hour! He took another quick sip and scooted down his palm tree, faster than you could say Jack Robinson! One more mouthful and he grabbed his bagpipes, scampered back up his palm tree and started playing, and the sound that came out was stupendous!

When Simon finally finished, the forest rang with applause from all animals, big and small.

Once Simon discovered this magic amber nectar, there was no stopping him. He became a world sensation almost overnight and played in all the top pop spots in the world, though his palm tree was always his favourite.

Basketmaker

Butcher

Carpenter

If you stop, sit quietly and listen, you might actually be lucky enough to hear Simon playing his pipes, drifting over the air! There's nothing like the sound of someone doing what they love.